Daddy, Me, and the
MAGIC HOUR

Laura Krauss Melmed

Illustrated by Sarita Rich

Sky Pony Press
New York

First Edition

Sky Pony Press books may be purchased in bulk at special discounts for sales promotion,
corporate gifts, fund-raising, or educational purposes. Special editions can also be created to
specifications. For details, contact the Special Sales Department, Sky Pony Press, 307 West
36th Street, 11th Floor, New York, NY 10018 or info@skyhorsepublishing.com.

Sky Pony® is a registered trademark of Skyhorse Publishing, Inc.®, a Delaware corporation.

Visit our website at www.skyponypress.com.

10 9 8 7 6 5 4 3 2 1

Manufactured in China, January 2018
This product conforms to CPSIA 2008

Library of Congress Cataloging-in-Publication Data is available on file.

Cover design by Kate Gartner
Cover illustration by Sarita Rich

Print ISBN: 978-1-5107-0791-7
Ebook ISBN: 978-1-5107-0795-5

WE'RE HOME!

THUD go our backpacks
on the front hall floor.

Daddy starts cooking,

while I run around like a super hero, yelling,

KA

and Mommy feeds the baby

Mommy says, "Please settle down."
And Daddy tells me, "Stop bothering the cat,
and come to the table. Now."

After supper, Daddy says,
"It's the Magic Hour!"
That's what we call it,
when we take our after-
supper walk.

The sun has gone down,
but clouds still show a sunny glow
as Mommy waves to us from the stoop.

Outside, bright,
loud daytime
is getting softer.
Some neighbors are out spraying hoses
on thirsty front yard roses
that are showing their colors
before darkness falls.

Here come the dogs
stepping out with their people
for a Magic Hour parade.

They don't bark at me,
and I am not afraid.

"Good job!" says Daddy,
when I pat a friendly one
who wags his tail a little and licks my face.

Thump, thump, thump, thump

Behind us two feet pound,
then the sound of hard breathing
as a jogger passes by.

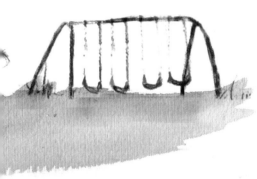

I run to the playground, hide,
and jump out with a giant **ROAR**

that scares a shout from Daddy.

Daddy tickles me

and I tickle him.

We laugh and laugh,
then, as we quiet down
we listen to the peaceful sound
of the playground at the Magic Hour
when we are almost the only ones around.

I can choose any swing I wan
Higher and higher I fly
until the toe of my sneaker
almost touches the sky.

Now Daddy is next to me.
Up and down and up we go,
exactly together,

and

together

we

slow.

Then we're heading home,
past a lady riding her bike.
She waves and smiles at us
and we wave back,
making a Magic Hour friend.

I hear crickets chirping
up in the treetops, where I can't see.

One firefly sparks,
and then more twinkle high and low.
Daddy teaches me how to catch one
in two hands,
hold it carefully, and then let it go.

The sky is purpling now.
Daddy shows me how things that are white by day,
like his shirt and my shoes,
and that patch of daisies,
glow all silvery as daytime fades away.

One swoop, and I'm up
on Daddy's shoulders.
Together, we make a quiet giant
who can almost reach the moon,
and by that round moon's light
we head home to Mommy,

where I give her a flower
and tell about the Magic Hour,
in my very hushest voice,
before she tucks me in for the
night.